HUSH LITTLE BABY

Based on a traditional lullaby

Illustrated by Turi MacCombie

Hush Little Baby. A Bantam Book/June 1989. All rights reserved. Copyright © 1989 by Parachute Press, Inc. Published by arrangement with Parachute Press, Inc. No part of this book may be reproduced or transmitted in any form or by any means, electronic or mechanical, including photocopying, recording, or by any information storage and retrieval system, without permission in writing from the publisher.

ISBN 0-553-15717-5

Published simultaneously in the United States and Canada. Bantam Books are sold by Bantam Books, a division of Bantam Doubleday Dell Publishing Group, Inc. Its trademark, consisting of the words "Bantam Books" and the portrayal of a rooster, is Registered in U.S. Patent and Trademark Office and in other countries. Marca Registrada. Bantam Books, 666 Fifth Avenue, New York, New York 10103. Printed in the United States of America.

0 9 8 7 6 5 4 3 2 1

BANTAM BOOKS

NEW YORK • TORONTO • LONDON • SYDNEY • AUCKLAND

Hush little baby,
don't say a word,
Mama's gonna buy you a ...

2

mockingbird.

If that mockingbird won't sing,
Mama's gonna buy you a . . .

5

diamond ring.

If that diamond ring is brass,
Mama's gonna buy you a . . .

7

looking glass.

If that looking glass gets broke,
Mama's gonna buy you a . . .

billy goat.

If that billy goat won't pull,
Mama's gonna buy you a . . .

cart and bull.

If that cart and bull turn over,
Mama's gonna buy you a . . .

dog named Rover.

If that dog named Rover won't bark,
Mama's gonna buy you a . . .

horse and cart.

If that horse and cart run away,
Mama's gonna buy you a . . .

little brown bay.

If that little brown bay won't budge,
Mama's gonna buy you some...

chocolate fudge.

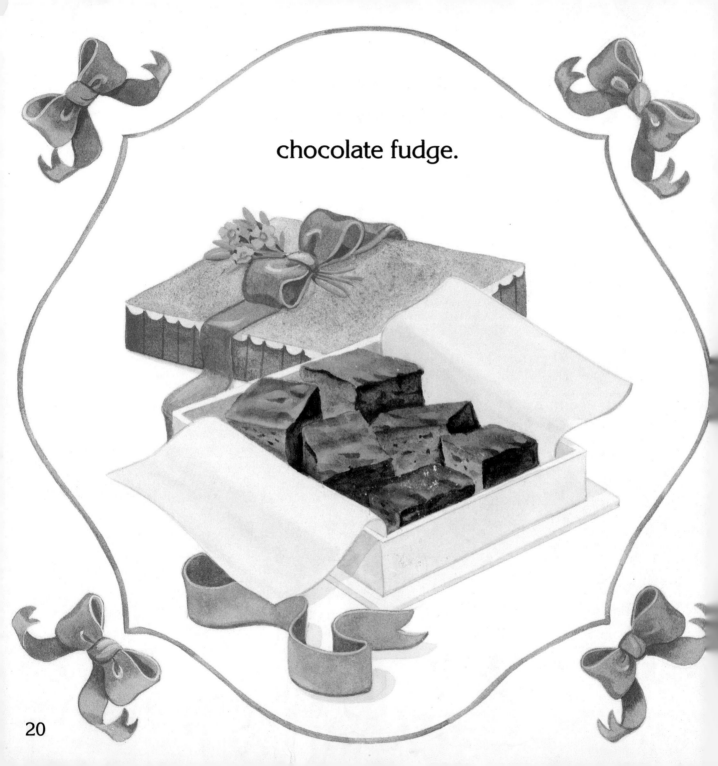

If that chocolate fudge falls down,
You'll still be the . . .

PRETTIEST BABY IN TOWN.

HUSH LITTLE BABY

Fast (♩ = 120)

Hush lit-tle ba - by, don't say a word, Ma-ma's gon-na buy you a mock-ing - bird.
If that_ mock-ing - bird won't_ sing, Ma-ma's gon-na buy you a dia-mond ring.

If that dia-mond ring is brass, Ma-ma's gon-na buy you a look- ing glass.
If that look - ing glass gets broke, Ma-ma's gon-na buy you a bil -ly goat.

If that bil - ly goat won't_ pull, Ma-ma's gon-na buy you a cart and bull.
If that cart and bull turn o - ver, Ma-ma's gon-na buy you a dog named Ro-ver.

If that dog named Ro-ver won't_ bark, Ma-ma's gon-na buy you a horse and cart.
If that horse and cart_ run a - way, Ma-ma's gon-na buy you a lit-tle brown bay.

If that lit - tle brown bay won't budge, Ma-ma's gon-na buy you some choc-o-late fudge.
If that choc-o - late fudge falls down, You'll still be the pret-ti - est ba- by in town.